Who's
for the
Zoo?

Two plays by
Jean Ure and Leonard Gregory

Illustrated by Mike Dodd

 LONGMAN

Who's For the Zoo?

The play is set in the classroom of Year 6 at Woodside School
The characters are
Miss Lilley, the Year 6 teacher

Girls
Catherine rather shy but cares deeply about things
Soozie Catherine's best friend, who always sticks up for her
Kelly small and very earnest
Jacky athletic and can be aggressive

The Spider Gang
Alison Gang leader and inclined to be bossy
Shirin second-in-command and thinks herself rather superior
Sophie outgoing and friendly
Collette Sophie's best friend, and a giggler

Boys
The Gang

All the Gang members play at being fierce. They quite often fig
amongst themselves.
Cameron
Billy
Darren
Ben Ben is more sensitive than the others but tries not to
show it
Nicky a live wire: the class clown
Kevin Kevin would love to be a Gang member but isn't quite
tough enough
Bader a quiet, clever boy who takes life very seriously

One person should read the stage directions which are in italic
type like this: *The curtain rises.*

Scene 1

The curtain rises to reveal an empty classroom, save for Miss Lilley seated at her desk.

The door suddenly opens and Year 6 come pouring in, chattering and pushing. The Gang – Cameron, Billy, Darren and Ben – are throwing punches at one another.

Miss Lilley *(clapping her hands)* All right, all right! Settle down, everyone! I have an important announcement to make.

The noise subsides slightly as people find their places.

Miss Lilley Right! That's better. Now, as you know, in three weeks' time it's going to be half term and we're all going on our outing. What we have to decide is where we're going to go. It obviously has to be something which ties in with our animal projects, so I thought either the Natural History Museum –

The Gang groan, loudly. Some of the others pull faces.

Miss Lilley (*raising her voice*) Or we can go to the Zoo.

The class are noisily enthusiastic. Table tops are thumped, feet stamped.

Cameron Yeah, the Zoo!

Others The Zoo!

Miss Lilley Let's have a show of hands. How many of you want to go to the Zoo?

All the class except Catherine put their hands up.

Miss Lilley That seems to be just about everybody. It looks as though the Zoo it is, then.

The class cheer.

Soozie Please, miss –

Miss Lilley Yes, Soozie?

Soozie Catherine didn't put her hand up, miss.

All the class turn to look at Catherine.

Miss Lilley Didn't you, Catherine? I must have missed that. So you'd rather go to the Natural History Museum?

Catherine nods, shyly.

Cameron No! We're going to the Zoo!

Alison We've already decided, miss.

Nicky We're going to see the monkeys!

Kelly And the snakes! I want to see the snakes! I want to see cobras!

Jacky I want to see water moccasins! Water moccasins is deadly.

Ben So's rattlers. Rattlers is even worse than water moccasins.

Cameron Black mambas is worse than anything.

Kevin   What about piranhas? I bet a shoal of piranhas could eat an elephant.

Collette   What do they feed them on, miss? The piranhas?

Miss Lilley I don't know, Colette. We'll have to find out.

Cameron   Elephants! They feed 'em on elephants!

A pause while the class think about this.

Catherine   *(speaking in a small voice)* In the Natural History Museum they have dinosaurs.

Miss Lilley Yes, they do, Catherine. That's quite true.

Ben   Yeah, but they're all dead, miss!

Darren   All fossils and stuff.

Miss Lilley Well, yes, that is also true. But imagine the thrill of seeing the skeletons of creatures that lived all those millions of years ago!

The class consider this.

Alison   It's more fun seeing live things.

Nicky   Yeah, fossils is boring.

Miss Lilley I'm afraid Catherine, you do seem to be in a minority.

Shirin   She's always in a minority.

Soozie   Don't you get on her case!

Miss Lilley All right! Let's not fall out. I know what we'll do. Before we have a final vote we'll read some of the poems we wrote last week. The ones about animals. I've still got them here. Sophie, would you give them out?

Sophie takes the poems from Miss Lilley and goes round the class with them.

Miss Lilley Who shall we start with? Cameron! You've got a big mouth. Let's start with you.

Cameron Me?

Miss Lilley Yes! You! Come on. Let's hear it. And announce it properly, please.

Cameron, deeply embarrassed, clears his throat.

Cameron   'The Yak.' *(he reads rather badly)*
The yak is black
Its name is Mac.
I sit on its back
On top of a sack
And whack the yak
To make it clack.

Pause

Miss Lilley   Did everyone like that? Catherine, what did you think about it?

Catherine   *(speaking apologetically)* I didn't like him whacking the yak very much.

The Gang and one or two others groan.

Miss Lilley I expect he didn't whack it too hard, did you, Cameron? Soozie! What about yours?

Soozie bounces up.

Soozie Yes, miss... 'The Panda.'
The panda is furry with big beady eyes,
Ringed all about with black.
It feeds on shoots of young bamboo.
That's all it eats.
Nothing else.
Not even packets of crisps or chewing gum.
It makes me glad that I'm not one!

Miss Lilley How about that, Catherine? Was that any better? Alison! I seem to remember yours was rather good. Let's hear yours.

Alison stands up, very self–important.

Alison 'The Hippopotamus' by Alison Webb.
The hippopotamus
Met an octopus
Down at the bottom of the sea.
The hippopotamus
Said to the octopus
"How come you have more arms than me?"

The class applaud and cheer.

Miss Lilley That was quite clever, wasn't it? Now, then, I think we'll have just one more. Can we have yours, please, Catherine?

Catherine *(speaking rather shyly)* 'Gorilla.'
A gorilla in the wild is free to run
  about and do just as he pleases.
Eat a nut or a berry,
Play and be merry,
All the day long.
But when a gorilla is kept in a cage
He can't run or play or even walk,
  hardly, or do anything at all.
And that, I think is wrong.

The class is silent.

Miss Lilley Well, what did you think of that?

The class murmur and nod their heads.

Sophie It was good.

Jacky   Yeah, it was.

Soozie   It was very good.

Bader   Very well written, miss.

Miss Lilley And how about what Catherine was actually saying? How many of you agree with her, that keeping animals in cages is wrong?

Slowly, hands go up. Soozie, Sophie, Colette, Kelly and some of the other girls, but not Alison, Shirin or Jacky.

Bader, Ben and Kevin put their hands up, and maybe one or two of the other boys, but not Cameron, Billy, Darren or Nicky.

Miss Lilley And the rest of you? I take it you don't agree? Tell us why!

Cameron   Animals is only animals. Not like human beings.

Miss Lilley Catherine? What do you say to that?

Catherine   It means it's worse for animals. If they were human beings they could think things to stop from getting bored, but if they're animals they can't do that. Animals only know about being free.

Cameron   Yeah, 'cos they're stupid!

Ben   Not nearly as stupid as you!

Cameron   You shut your –

Miss Lilley Ben and Cameron, stop that this instant. Who else has any views? Bader?

Bader   *(speaking very seriously)* I think zoos are all right if they're breeding animals and putting them back in the wild, but not just for people to look at. And not kept in cages.

Collette   What they ought to have is big parks where they can roam about.

Billy   But if they was in parks, you couldn't go and look at 'em. Not like you can in zoos.

Soozie   Of course you could!

Billy   Well, you can't, 'cos we went to this place once where they was all supposed to be walking about and we didn't see a thing, hardly.

Darren   Yeah, that's right. It's really boring just driving round and not seeing nothing. At least if they're in cages you can get a good look at 'em.

Catherine   How would you like to be in a cage with people standing there gawping at you?

Darren   Smashing! I bet they'd all take photographs.

Billy   Yeah, and feed you buns and stuff!

Catherine   *(so angry she's nearly crying)* Stupid! You're just STUPID!

Cameron   What's she getting all uptight about? They're only animals.

Catherine   They've got feelings, haven't they? Same as you?

Ben   He ain't got no feelings.

Catherine   You want to see what it's like, being locked up!

Cameron   Nobody gonna lock me up. Have to catch me first!

Cameron jumps up from his chair. Ben jumps up after him.

Miss Lilley Sit down, sit down! I've had an idea. I think
we'll play the zoo game ...

Curtain down (or blackout).

* * *

Scene 2

*As the lights come up we see that the classroom has been
turned into a zoo.*

*Tables have been turned on their sides, with their legs
against the wall, to make cages. Chairs have been used to
make enclosures. A rubber paddling pool has been
borrowed from the Infants for the hippopotamus to wallow
in.*

*There is a large notice pinned to the classroom door saying
"Woodside Zoo" Notices saying "Lions", "Tigers",
"Monkeys", etc., are pinned to the cages.*

*Some of the class are still putting the finishing touches to
the cages. Some are running about pretending to be
animals: Nicky is being a monkey; Billy and Darren are
being tigers, and roaring; Jacky is jumping, being a
kangaroo.*

Miss Lilley Come on, then, pay attention! All of you who
agreed with Catherine, stand over here by me.
All the rest of you … into your cages! Go on,
Nicky, there's the monkey house! Who was the
kangaroo? Jacky? Cameron, you were the yak.
Alison? What were you?

Alison Can't remember, miss. I'll be a panther.

Ben That wasn't what you wrote your poem about!
You wrote about a hippopotamus.

Alison *(speaking angrily)* Doesn't mean I've got to be
one!

Miss Lilley Oh, yes, it does, I'm afraid! Off you go and
jump in your paddling pool. Bader, will you be
zoo keeper and keep all these animals in order
for us? I want you all to be on your best
behaviour. Remember, you're animals in a zoo
and people are coming to look at you.

Miss Lilley goes out, with Catherine and her supporters.

The animals, enjoying themselves, jump, waddle and hop in their cages.

Cameron   What's a yak do? I don't know what a yak does.

Bader   You shouldn't have chosen it, then.

Cameron   I want to be something else! I want to be a hyena!

Bader   Well, you can't. You're a yak. Just be quiet or I'll whack you.

The door opens and Miss Lilley comes in with the visitors, walking neatly in a crocodile.

Miss Lilley   Here we are at the Zoo! Come to see the animals. Now –

She stops at the monkey cage, full of monkeys.

Miss Lilley   What have we here?

Sophie   *(reading the notice)* Monkeys, miss.

The visitors stand watching as the monkeys perform various monkey tricks.

Ben   Call themselves monkeys? They're rubbish!

Kevin   I never knew monkeys picked their noses, miss.

Ben   It's probably got a flea.

Collette   What, up its nose?

Ben   Why not? Get 'em anywhere.

Collette   Ugh!

Kevin   I once saw one with a red bum.

Soozie   Bet it wasn't as ugly as this lot!

Miss Lilley   Don't get too close to them, Soozie, they might bite. Let's move on and see something else.

Kelly   The kangaroo!

The kangaroo jumps obligingly in its cage.

Miss Lilley   What do you think of it?

Ben   Not a lot.

Kevin   Doesn't jump very high, does it?

Sophie   I thought they jumped much higher than that.

The kangaroo increases its efforts.

Soozie	Pathetic!
Jacky	*(speaking crossly)* I could jump right out of this cage if I wanted!
Miss Lilley	Nobody jumps out of any cages. It's against the rules. Let's go and look at the next one.
Nicky	*(calling from the monkey cage)* Hey, miss! Can we get out now?
Miss Lilley	Certainly not. You stay where you are. Animals in zoos do not get out of their cages. They are put there and they stay there. Now, what's this? The hippopotamus.

The hippopotamus is sitting sulking by the side of its paddling pool.

Sophie   Ugh!

Soozie   Gross.

Collette   Like a big pig.

Catherine   *(speaking seriously)* I think mainly the hippopotamus is a water animal.

Soozie   Why isn't it in its water, then? Get in your pool, you horrid ugly thing!

Kevin   Go on, fatty! Move!

Alison   Get lost!

Sophie   Ooh! Did you hear that, miss?

Ben   It hasn't half got a big mouth.

Kevin   Big body, an' all.

Sophie   *(poking at the hippo)* Do something, fatso!

Miss Lilley I shouldn't poke at it, Sophie. It might not like it.

Soozie   Wonder if it's got a name?

Sophie   You got a name, fatty?

Ben   Yeah, it's called Alison.

Soozie   Hallo, fat Alison!

(The hippo springs to its feet)

Alison   Any more of that and I'll smash you one.

Soozie   Ooh! Nasty!

Miss Lilley Zoo Keeper, your hippopotamus seems to be getting out of control.

Bader   I'll see to it, don't worry!

Bader rushes across to the hippo and attempts to push it into its paddling pool. The hippo fights back.

Miss Lilley Let's move on.

Nicky   Miss!

Miss Lilley takes no notice

Miss Lilley What's this funny-looking creature?

Nicky Miss, this cage ain't big enough, miss!

Ben It says it's a yak.

The yak makes a loud barking noise.

Nicky and fellow monkeys Miss! Miss!

Sophie Doesn't sound much like a yak to me.

Cameron How do you know what a yak sounds like?

Sophie Well, it doesn't sound like a dog, I know that!

In the background, the monkeys make an attempt to climb out of their cage. Bader races across and beats them back.

Bader Stop that!

Bader then rushes back to battle with the hippo.

Soozie We could always whack it.

Miss Lilley There will be no touching of the animals, Soozie. Some of them are quite fierce.

Ben Yeah, and some of them don't know what they're supposed to be doing.

The visitors move away. Bader is still wrestling with the hippo. In the tiger cage, the tigers start to punch each other.

Cameron I never asked to be a yak!

Catherine Miss, the tigers are fighting.

Miss Lilley So they are! Look, everyone! Look at the tigers!

All the visitors turn to look at the tigers in their cage. Embarrassed, the tigers stop their punching.

Kelly What were they fighting about, miss?

Miss Lilley Territory, I expect. It's the sort of thing that happens when animals are kept in unnatural conditions ... they quite often turn on each other.

Darren It was his fault! He started it!

Billy I never! You kicked me!

Darren   Yeah, 'cos you trod on my foot, you great nerd!

Billy   I couldn't help it! There ain't enough room in here!

The visitors turn away.

Catherine   It's terrible, keeping tigers shut in a cage.

Sophie   They shouldn't really be in zoos, should they, miss? Not tigers.

Catherine   Not any animals.

Sophie   But specially big ones.

Darren   *(speaking to Billy)* You do that again and I'll bop you one!

Bader   Stop fighting, you two!

Bader, who has at last pushed the hippo into its paddling pool, races across to the tiger cage. As he does so, the bell rings for lunch.

Kelly   Look, miss, there are penguins over there.

Miss Lilley   Yes, I see them, Kelly, but I'm afraid we don't have time for them at the moment. We shall have to leave the penguins until later. Zoo Keeper, are you going to come and have your lunch? You needn't worry about the animals, they won't be going anywhere. They're locked in their cages. And they can't get out, can they? They're prisoners. So they can just stay put while the rest of us go off.

Loud shouts of protest from the animals. As Miss Lilley and the visitors move towards the door, all the animals begin climbing out of their cages to join them.

Miss Lilley *stops and turns.*

Miss Lilley Darren – Cameron – where do you think you're going?

Cameron ⎫
           }together Get some grub, miss.
Darren ⎭   Bell's gone, miss.

Miss Lilley I thought I made myself clear. We, the visitors, are going to have our lunch. You are going to stay where you are. You are wild animals. We can't have you rampaging round the canteen frightening people. You'll have to wait till feeding time.

Billy   When's that, miss?

Miss Lilley I don't know but probably not for ages.

Cameron   That ain't fair!

Billy   I'm hungry, miss!

Nicky   Miss, I'm bored!

Miss Lilley I'm sorry, Nicky. I'm sorry, all of you. That's the way it is ... you're animals, in a zoo. Animals in zoos do get bored. And it isn't fair, I quite agree. Now, get back to your cages!

The animals mutter, restively.

Jacky   *Please,* miss –

Alison   I want my lunch, miss.

Billy   So do I, miss.

Jacky   Please, miss –

Cameron   Miss, I'm *STARVING!*

Jacky   I want to go somewhere, miss.

Miss Lilley Do I take it that you are tired of being animals in the zoo?

Animals   Yeah!

Miss Lilley How many of you want to stop being animals and have lunch?

All their hands go up.

Miss Lilley Well, in that case I think we'd better put the chairs and tables back. But before we do, let's just have one final vote, to make sure ... who's for the zoo?

There is a pause while everyone thinks.

Shirin I'm just about sick of zoos.

Cameron Yeah, I am an' all.

Shirin Sick of everything about them.

Miss Lilley What exactly are you trying to tell me?

Cameron Don't want to go to no zoo.

Miss Lilley So where would you prefer to go? The Natural History Museum?

Another pause.

Nicky They got dinosaurs in the Natural History Museum.

Darren Yeah, and fossils and stuff.

Nicky Be quite interesting, seeing a dinosaur.

Billy And all them skelingtons from years ago.

Darren All the dead stuff.

Kelly They got tyrannosauruses in there, miss?

Cameron And pterodactyls? I want to see a pterodactyl!

Darren I want to see a mammoth!

Billy   I want to see a sabre-toothed tiger!

Billy and Darren make mammoth noises and sabre-toothed tiger noises at each other.

Miss Lilley So let's get this settled once and for all ... are we going to the Zoo –

There is silence for a moment.

Miss Lilley Or are we going to the Natural History Museum?

All hands shoot into the air.

Everybody Yeah!

* * *

Loud Mouth

A play in eleven scenes (adapted by Jean Ure and Leonard Gregory from the book of the same name published by Orchard Books.)

The scene is set mainly in the playground of Woodside Junior School.

The characters are

Miss Lilley, the Year 6 teacher
Mrs Shanks, Leonie's mother

Girls
Leonie
Jacky
Alison
Shirin
Sophie
Colette
Soozie
Catherine
Pavindra

Boys
Cameron
Billy
Darren
Ben

One person should read the stage directions, which are in *italic* type.

The action of the play takes place mainly in the playground of Woodside Junior School.

Scene 1

The lights come up on the playground full of children. Boys are kicking footballs, girls are talking in groups.

Leonie appears, proudly wheeling her bicycle through the school gates. It is winter and she is wearing ear muffs. One of the boys kicks a football perilously close to the bicycle.

Leonie   Watch my new bike!

A group of girls turns to look.

Alison   *(imitating Leonie)* Watch my new bike!

Darren   Give it a kick!

Darren aims a kick at the bike. Leonie screams.

Leonie   Stop it! You'll mark it!

Alison   Stop it! You'll mark it!

The other girls giggle.

Shirin   Stupid nit.

Cameron and his gang (Billy, Darren and Ben) surround Leonie.

Cameron   What's your problem?

Leonie shrinks back.

Leonie   It's new.

Cameron   So what?

Leonie   My mum'll be cross if anything happens to it.

Cameron   Who said anything's going to happen to it?

Leonie   It will if you kick it.

Darren   Kick what I like.

Darren aims another kick at the bike as the Gang move off with their football. Leonie, rather scared, turns to put her bike in the bike shed. Sophie breaks away from the group of girls and eagerly runs across.

Sophie   Leonie! Can I have a go on it?

Leonie hesitates.

Sophie   Please! Can I?

Leonie   You'd better not. You might bash it into something.

Sophie   I wouldn't! I promise! I know how to ride a bike.

Leonie   Yes, but this is new. It was very expensive. It's one of the best sort of bikes that you can buy.

Other girls have come over to join them.

Jacky   Looks just like an ordinary sort of bike to me.

Leonie   Well, it's not. It's a special one.

Jacky   Why? What's special about it?

Alison   Just because it's hers. Everything she has
               always is.

Sophie   What are you doing now?

Leonie   Locking it up. I've got a special secret padlock.
               It's got a secret combination, like a safe. You
               have to click it round till you get the right
               number.

Leonie stands there, clicking. The others watch.

Leonie   I mustn't tell anyone what the numbers are
               because then they could open the padlock and
               steal the bike.

Sophie   Suppose you forgot them?

Leonie   I can't forget them. I've got a special secret
               way of remembering.

Leonie pulls open the padlock and triumphantly snaps it round the front wheel of her bike.

Leonie   Do you want to know what it is?

Jacky   Not particularly.

Leonie   It's ever so easy. All I do, I just say FIDO ... and then I remember. The reason it's secret is that I'm the only one that knows what it means. You could say FIDO as much as you like and the bike wouldn't move. But if I say it –

Alison   Say it.

Leonie   Not now. I've put it away now. And anyway, the bell's gone.

The girls move off, Sophie, Jacky and Pavindra slightly behind.

Sophie   I don't see how just saying FIDO can make a padlock come open.

Pavindra   It's the letters. You have to turn them into numbers.

Sophie   How?

Pavindra   You have to work it out, with the alphabet ...A, B, C, until you get to F. Then I. Then –

Jacky   Like a code. Stupid loud mouth! Now she's gone and told us!

* * *

Scene 2

A group of girls in the playground at break.

Alison   I'm just about sick of Leonie Shanks. *(she imitates Leonie)* Look at my new dress – look at my new shoes –

Shirin   Look at my new pencil case –

Soozie   Look at my new ear muffs –

Shirin   Makes you want to spit!

Alison   It's about time we did something.

Collette   What sort of something?

Alison   Something to stop her.

Sophie   Stop her talking?

Alison   Stop her showing off.

A pause while they think about it.

Sophie   How?

Alison   We could have a society ... a Hate Leonie Shanks society.

Collette   What would it do?

Soozie   Hate Leonie Shanks!

Collette   Yes, but what would it do?

Shirin   Not speak to her. Not until she stopped
showing off.

Alison   Let's vote. Hands up everyone who thinks it's
a good idea.

*Everyone except Sophie, Pavindra and Catherine put their
hands up.*

Alison   Now hands up everyone who doesn't think it's
a good idea.

The three put their hands up.

Alison   That's it. You're outnumbered.

Shirin   Right. I vote anyone talks to her from now on
gets sent to Coventry.

Shirin looks hard at the three.

Alison   *(speaking to Catherine)* Dunno why you want to talk to her, anyway ... her and her mink ear muffs. I thought you didn't approve of people wearing animal fur?

Catherine   They're not really mink. She was just pretending.

Shirin   Just boasting, you mean. Like always.

Soozie   If she goes on about her new bike again I shall scream.

Leonie joins them.

Leonie   I'm going to go and look at my new bike.

Soozie screams. Several of the girls giggle. Leonie tries to take no notice.

Leonie   Who wants to come with me?

Sophie begins to move forward, then remembers and stops. There is a silence.

Leonie   I expect I shall take the padlock off. Probably.

Alison   Let's go and see if our bulbs are doing anything.

They all move off except Catherine, who hesitates.

Catherine   I'm really s–

Soozie   C'mon!

*Soozie grabs Catherine by the arm and pulls her away.
They all run off, leaving Leonie on her own. Leonie tries
hard not to care. After a moment or two, she goes across
to the bike shed, where she finds the Gang awaiting her.
Leonie begins to back away, but they quickly surround her.*

Cameron   We want a go on that bike.

Leonie   *(scared)* You can't! It's new!

Billy indicates the padlock.

Billy   How's this padlock work?

Leonie   I can't tell you. It's a secret.

Darren   You'd better tell us, 'cause if you don't –

Cameron   We'll kick your spokes in.

Cameron raises a foot to kick.

Leonie   No! Please!

*She tries to stop them, but Cameron shakes her off and
aims a mighty kick at the bike. Leonie cries out.*

Cameron   Well? You gonna tell us how it works?

Leonie is silent.

Ben   You'd better.

*Ben is not as big a bully as the others. He is not so much
threatening Leonie as advising her for her own good.*

Ben   Then nobody'll get hurt.

Billy   That's right. All we want's a go on the bike.

Cameron raises his foot again.

Cameron   So? You gonna tell us or –

Leonie   It's FIDO.

Cameron   FIDO?

Darren   What's FIDO?

Leonie   *(in a whisper)* Letters of the alphabet.

Billy   What's she on about?

Ben   You undo it for us ... go on!

Leonie bends down and unlocks the padlock. Cameron instantly snatches the bike, jumps on it and cycles off stage. Leonie watches, in anguish.

As Cameron cycles back, Darren seizes the bike and also rides off. Billy is next, but Billy is not a very good rider. As he cycles off there is a thump and a yell. Leonie rushes forward.

Leonie   My bike! Look what you've done to my bike!

Billy reappears, back on the bike and wobbling all over the place.

Billy   I ain't done nothing to your stupid bike!

He jumps off it and throws it down. Leonie examines it.

Leonie   You have! You've made a mark! You've scratched it!

Ben   It's not very much. Put a bit of paint on it and it won't even show.

Leonie is almost in tears.

Leonie   I haven't got any paint!

Darren   Well, get some, then!

Leonie   But my mother will see it –

Cameron moves in on her.

Cameron   You tell your mum and we'll do you.

Leonie   But she'll ask me! She'll want to know how it happened.

Darren   So what are you gonna tell her?

Leonie bites her lip.

Billy   You're gonna tell her you had a little accident, aren't you?

Cameron   That's right! You are, aren't you? Gonna say you had an accident.

Slowly, Leonie nods.

* * *

Scene 3

The end of the school day. Leonie's mum is waiting for her just inside the gates as Leonie wheels her bike out. The Gang are hovering nearby.

Mum   Leonie! What's happened to your lovely new bike?

Mum bends down to examine it. The Gang move in closer.

Leonie   I –

Leonie looks at the Gang.

Leonie   I scraped it.

Mum   Already? That's very careless! Daddy's not going to be at all happy about that. This was a very expensive bicycle, you know. Daddy had to pay a lot of money for it.

Leonie   Yes, I know.

Mum   You must take better care of it, Leonie! Money doesn't grow on trees.

Mum rubs at the mark.

Mum   We'll have to get some paint on it before Daddy sees it.

Mum straightens up.

Mum   So what did the other girls think? Did they like it?

Leonie   I suppose so.

Mum   Only suppose so? What did they say?

Leonie   Said they liked it.

Mum   Well, there you are, then!

Pause, as Leonie takes the bike from Mum.

Leonie	Jacky Gibbs said it looked just like any ordinary sort of bike.
Mum	Well, you can tell Jacky Gibbs that it most certainly isn't any ordinary sort of bike!
Leonie	I told her.
Mum	And she didn't believe you?

Leonie shakes her head.

Mum	I shouldn't take any notice if I were you. She's probably just jealous.
Leonie	Perhaps I oughtn't to use it for going to school on?
Mum	Nonsense! Of course you must use it. You can't let a jealous little girl put you off.
Leonie	But it might get messed up ... if it rains or anything.
Mum	Don't worry! I wouldn't let you use it if it rained. The pavements might be slippy.

As Leonie and her mum start to go off, Cameron leaps forward.

Cameron	Hey, missis! Can we have a go on that bike?

Leonie's mum freezes.

Mum   Are you in the habit of addressing people as missis? I'm Leonie's mum and my name is Mrs Shanks. And no, you certainly may not have a go on Leonie's bike!

Leonie and her mum go off. The Gang leap and dance exultantly.

Cameron   My name is Mrs Shanks –

Ben   And you certainly may not have a go on Leonie's bike!

The Gang fall about laughing.

* * *

Scene 4

The following morning, at the playground gates. People are playing in the playground as Leonie's mum accompanies her to school.

Mum   So which one is the jealous little girl?

Leonie looks across the playground. At that moment, Jacky runs past chased by Sophie.

Leonie   I don't think she's here.

Mum   That's a pity. I'd have liked a word with her. Right! Off you go. I'll just stay and watch you put your bike away.

Leonie wheels her bike to the bike shed. Miss Lilley, the class teacher, is there, putting her own bike away.

Miss Lilley   My goodness, Leonie! That's a very splendid machine you have there.

Leonie waves goodbye to her mum and walks across the playground to where Soozie and Catherine are frightening each other with a black rubber snake, throwing it at each other and screeching.

Leonie   I've got one of those. Only mine's bigger than that ... I should think mine's probably a python.

Catherine is about to say something when Soozie throws the snake at her.

Leonie   You can get them at that stall down the market. They've got hundreds of them ... snakes and frogs and lizardy things. I've got a big furry spider. It's huge. It looks just like a real one. It cost ever such a lot.

Soozie and Catherine take no notice of her. Leonie, growing desperate, moves across to Pavindra, who is standing there watching them.

Leonie   I've got a big spider, *AND* a snake. If I brought them in, we could play with them.

Pavindra looks scared and doesn't say anything.

Leonie   Shall I? My snake's much better than their one.

The bell rings and the pupils line up to go into school. The Gang jostle and push at Leonie. Cameron yanks her hair.

Cameron   Ha ha! Leonie Sheepshanks!

Darren   We'll have another go at the bike later.

The Gang move into line with the other boys from their class. Leonie moves into line with the girls, next to Jacky.

Jacky   Pooh! I smell something nasty.

Jacky makes a great show of turning round, her nose pinched between finger and thumb.

Jacky   Ugh! Sheepshanks! No wonder!

Jacky rushes off, further down the line. The others, also holding their noses, all shuffle as far away from Leonie as possible. Leonie is left on her own, struggling with tears.

Lights fade.

* * *

Scene 5

Playtime the same day. Catherine, Soozie and Jacky have been to feed the rabbits. They pass the bike shed on their way back into the playground. Catherine and Soozie, deep in conversation, walk on, but Jacky lingers by Leonie's bike. Lovingly she strokes a finger over it. She tries the handlebars, tries the brakes, rings the bell. Then she bends down and looks at the padlock. We see her working out the combination on her fingers.

Jacky   A – B – C – D – E – F –

She hesitates, knowing that what she is doing is wrong but unable to resist the temptation. Jacky begins to undo the padlock as Leonie comes into the playground. Leonie shrieks and rushes over to her.

Leonie   *(screaming)* What are you doing with my bike? You leave my bike alone!

Miss Lilley hears the noise and comes across to investigate.

Miss Lilley   Leonie? What's the matter?

Leonie   She's a thief! She was trying to steal my bike! 'Cause she's jealous –

Jacky   I wasn't trying to steal your bike! I was looking at it, that's all.

Leonie   You weren't! You were touching it! You were trying to open the padlock!

Jacky   I wasn't! I just wanted to see how it worked.

Leonie   Look! You've made a mark! You've scraped it!

Miss Lilley   Did you do that, Jacky?

Jacky   No, I did not!

Leonie   You did! You must have done!

Jacky   Well, I didn't!

Miss Lilley   You are quite sure of that, Jacky?

Jacky   Yes, I am!

Miss Lilley   All right, well, just keep away from Leonie's bike in future. We don't want any trouble, do we?

Jacky runs off with a glance of hatred at Leonie.

Miss Lilley   I'm sorry about the mark, Leonie, but if Jacky said she didn't do it ... are you quite sure it wasn't there before?

Leonie   *(muttering)* It might have been.

Miss Lilley   All it needs is a dab of paint. That'll cover it up.

As Leonie goes back across the playground she hears Jacky.

Jacky   ... said I was trying to steal it!

Alison   Cheek!

Shirin   Look, there she goes ... little Miss Show Off!

Leonie rushes back into school. As she goes through the doors the Gang are coming out. They jostle her and shove.

Cameron   Sheepshanks! Leonie Sheepshanks!

They dance round her, pushing her from one to another.

Billy   Let's go and beat up her new bike!

The Gang race boisterously into the playground. Leonie disappears into school.

* * *

Scene 6

The end of school, the same day. Leonie's Mum is waiting at the gates. Leonie wheels her bike towards her. They turn and start moving off.

Mum   Had a good day?

Leonie   Jacky Gibbs tried to steal my bike.

Mum   Leonie! Did you tell Miss Lilley?

Leonie   *(nodding)* Mm.

Mum   What did she say?

Leonie   She didn't say anything.

Mum   I think we'd better go and have a word with Miss Lilley ...

Mum turns and marches Leonie back into the school.

Scene 7

Lunch time, the following day. Miss Lilley is in the playground talking to a group of girls. The Gang, as usual, are kicking a football.

Suddenly Leonie comes running out of school, distraught and screaming. She is screaming so loudly that her words are not quite clear.

Leonie   My ear muffs! Someone's stolen my ear muffs!

Miss Lilley hurries towards her.

Miss Lilley Calm down, Leonie! I can't understand you. What are you trying to say?

Leonie is sobbing and hiccuping.

Leonie   My ear muffs ... someone's stolen my ear muffs!

Miss Lilley Your ear muffs? Are you absolutely certain that you were wearing your ear muffs?

Leonie   I had them on when I came to school!

Shirin   I suppose it was the mink ones?

Miss Lilley is alarmed.

Miss Lilley Mink?

Catherine They're not really mink. Only pretend.

Miss Lilley   Oh! That's a relief. Still, we must try to find them. Where did you put them, Leonie?

Leonie   I h-hung them over my p-peg and now they're n-not there!

Miss Lilley   Does anybody remember seeing Leonie's ear muffs?

All the girls shake their heads. Miss Lilley takes Leonie by the hand.

Miss Lilley   Let's go back and have a thorough search. You'll probably find they've just fallen on the floor.

Leonie and Miss Lilley go back into school.

Cameron   Stupid old Sheepshanks!

He kicks the ball and the Gang go roaring off.

Alison   Serve her right if someone has taken them.

Shirin   These are my *EAR* muffs that I was given at *CHRISTMAS.*

Shirin makes a loud being-sick noise.

Soozie   They were *EVER* so expensive.

Sophie   Real mink!

Sophie giggles.

Shirin   This is my new *DRESS* –

Collette   These are my new *SHOES* –

Soozie   This is my new *HANDKERCHIEF* –

Soozie pretends to blow her nose.

Alison   Pity someone doesn't take My New Bicycle.
That'd give her something to think about.

Jacky   I bet she'd try and blame me. I bet she thinks I took her stupid ear muffs.

Miss Lilley reappears with a tearful Leonie.

Miss Lilley Well, I'm afraid there doesn't seem to be any sign of them. I take it none of you girls borrowed them, just to try them on, and forgot to put them back?

Leonie looks hard at Jacky.

Jacky   I haven't touched them! I didn't even know they were there.

Miss Lilley It's all right, Jacky. No one is accusing you.

Jacky   She is!

Miss Lilley I'm sure she's not, are you, Leonie?

Leonie   She tried to steal my new bike.

Jacky   I never! I was only –

Miss Lilley Now, now, come on, you two! There's no need for that. Come with me, Leonie. We'd better go and make a formal report to the office.

Miss Lilley and Leonie go off again.

Jacky   Horrible thing! I'm not ever going to talk to her again!

* * *

The end of the school day by the bike sheds. Leonie is undoing her padlock. Sophie stops, on her way out of school.

Sophie   *(feeling awkward)* I'm sorry about your ear muffs.

Leonie   No, you're not! You're glad someone's taken them.

Sophie   *(hurt)* I'm not glad. But it wasn't very nice to accuse Jacky.

Leonie   She shouldn't have touched my bike.

Sophie   She was only interested. Everybody's interested. 'Cause it's a good bike. If you'd just let people have a go on it –

Leonie wheels her bike out of the shed.

Leonie   I'm not allowed to.

Leonie wheels the bike to the gates, where her Mum is waiting. Mum looks at Sophie.

Mum   Is that the little girl that's jealous?

Scene 9

The following day, alongside the woods. Jacky wanders on, on her way to school. We hear Leonie's voice, offstage.

Leonie   ... pulled me off my bike.

Jacky stops.

Leonie   *(offstage)* I fell over in the mud and hurt myself.

Jacky steps off the path and peers into the woods.

Jacky   That you, Leonie?

Leonie appears, looking frightened.

Leonie   *(babbling)* Someone knocked me off my bicycle and I fell in the mud and hurt myself.

There is a pause. Jacky obviously doesn't believe her.

Leonie   *(growing desperate)* I don't know who it was because I couldn't see them, but they came up behind me and knocked me off, and they took my bike and –

Jacky suddenly plunges past Leonie and into the woods. She reappears dragging Leonie's bike.

Jacky   What's this, then?

Leonie gives a pretend squeak of surprise.

Leonie   It's my bike!

Jacky   Surprise, surprise.

Jacky lets the bike fall to the ground.

Jacky   I suppose you were going to say it was me that took it?

Leonie   *(in a whisper)* No.

Jacky   So what d'you go and hide it for?

Leonie is silent. Jacky suddenly spies something else. She dives into the bushes.

Jacky   What's this?

Jacky reappears clutching a plastic bag. Leonie snatches at it but Jacky whisks it away. She opens it and takes out a pair of ear muffs.

Jacky   Ear muffs! You stole your own ear muffs!

Leonie cringes away from her.

Jacky   I don't get it. What's the game?

Leonie stays silent.

Jacky   I know! It was to get me into trouble, wasn't it?

Leonie   It wasn't! Honestly, it wasn't!

Jacky   So what d'you do it for?

Leonie   I thought –

Jacky   What?

Leonie   I thought ... people wouldn't hate me so much.

Jacky   You mean ... if everything got stolen?

Leonie nods. Jacky stares at her.

Leonie   *(in a whisper)* I suppose you're going to tell everyone?

Jacky   What makes you think that? *(angry)* It might be what you'd do. It's not necessarily what I'd do. What d'you take me for? Some kind of sneak? As well as a thief? I wasn't trying to steal your rotten bicycle!

Leonie   I know.

Jacky   And I never made that mark on it!

Leonie   I know.

Jacky   Well, then –

Silence.

Jacky   You'd better wipe some of that mud off.

*Jacky pulls a packet of paper hankies from her school bag
and does her best to clean her up. Leonie stands, helpless.*

Jacky   It's not very good, You'll have to say you fell
          off. Here.

Jacky hands Leonie the bag with the ear muffs.

Jacky   You can always tell Miss you made a mistake
          about the ear muffs ... say you found them at
          home.

Leonie backs away.

Leonie   I don't want them! You have them.

*Jacky is tempted. She tries them on, then reluctantly puts
them back in the bag.*

Jacky   Better not. I wouldn't mind a ride on your bike,
          though!

* * *

Scene 10

A few minutes later. Jacky and Leonie come through the school gates into the playground: Jacky is riding the bike. Alison and Shirin, who have just come in, stop to stare.

Alison   What happened to her?

Jacky   She fell off. We're just going to go and get her cleaned up. Later on, if people want, they can have a ride on her bike. Isn't that right? People can have a go on your bike?

Leonie nods, shyly.

Jacky   See?

She rides over to the cycle rack as the lights fade.

* * *

Scene II

The playground, at break. Sophie comes riding in on Leonie's bike from the direction of the school gardens. The others are queuing up. Leonie is there, with Jacky.

Sophie   Hey, Leonie! It's a really good bike!

Shirin   *(snatching at the bike)* My turn, my turn!

The Gang come swaggering up and shove their way to the head of the queue.

Cameron   I'll have some of that!

Jacky places herself in front of him.

Jacky   You will not, Cameron Philips! This is our bike. We don't want you lot messing about with it.

Cameron   Who says?

Jacky   I do!

Darren   What's it got to do with you?

Billy   It ain't your bike!

Sophie   No, it's Leonie's and she doesn't want you
riding it, do you?

Leonie   No, 'cause they make marks on it.

Alison   So just shove off!

The girls turn on the Gang, who go mumbling off, defeated, across the playground.

Cameron   Stupid Sheepshanks!

Alison   You wash your mouth out!

As Sophie hands the bike to Shirin, Jacky turns to Leonie.

Jacky   They give you any hassle, you just come to me.

Jacky slips her arm through Leonie's.

Jacky   I know how to deal with that lot!

* * *